P9-BZY-238

JACKRABBIT'S TALE

by Trish Kline

Illustrated by Fred Smith

This book is dedicated to my wife, Jackie, whose support and patience has made my illustration career possible — F.S.

© 2002 Trudy Corporation and the Smithsonian Institution, Washington DC 20560.

Published by Soundprints Division of Trudy Corporation, Norwalk, Connecticut.

All rights reserved. No part of this book may be reproduced or transmitted in any form or by any means whatsoever without prior written permission of the publisher.

Book design: Marcin D. Pilchowski
Editor: Laura Gates Galvin
Editorial assistance: Chelsea Shriver

First Edition 2002
10 9 8 7 6 5 4 3 2
Printed in China

Acknowledgments:
    Our very special thanks to Dr. Don E. Wilson of the Department of Systematic Biology at the Smithsonian Institution's National Museum of Natural History for his curatorial review.
    Soundprints would also like to thank Ellen Nanney and Robyn Bissette at the Smithsonian Institution's Office of Product Development and Licensing for their help in the creation of this book.

*Library of Congress Cataloging-in-Publication Data is
on file with the publisher and the Library of Congress.*

Table of Contents

A note to the reader:
Throughout this story you will see words in **bold letters**.
There is more information about these words in the
glossary. The glossary is in the back of the book.

Chapter 1

Night on the Prairie

The sun is setting. Soon it will be night. Many animals are going to their nests and **burrows**. It is time for them to sleep. Jackrabbit sleeps during the day.

Jackrabbit has been sleeping in a bush. While other animals sleep, she looks for food. Slowly, she pokes her nose out. She sniffs the air for the smell of foxes and coyotes. They are her **predators**.

Jackrabbit lifts her long ears. She points them straight up. She turns them. She listens for the sounds of predators walking in the brush. She listens for the sounds of predators in the air.

Jackrabbit does not sense danger. She creeps out from beneath the bush. She takes a few hops. She stops and listens for danger. No danger is near.

Soon it will be dark. Jackrabbit is not the only animal awake. She is not the only hungry animal, either. Jackrabbit is always alert.

Chapter 2
Fast Food

Jackrabbit loves to eat! She eats all night long. She likes to eat many plants. But, Jackrabbit likes grass best!

Jackrabbit goes to a **pasture**. It is her favorite place to eat. Her two front teeth have two more teeth right behind them. Her teeth are perfect for nibbling grass close to the ground.

Jackrabbit hears something. Her hearing is very good. She stands still. A fox is slowly creeping toward her. Jackrabbit lies quietly on the ground with her ears flat on her back. She stays as still as she can.

But the fox has seen her!
He is going to attack!
Jackrabbit jumps up and
hops away. Five feet. Ten
feet. Then she runs fast.
Where should she run?
Where is the fox? Can
she get away?

Jackrabbit runs around bushes. She zigzags across pastures. The fox is fast, but tonight he can not catch Jackrabbit. The fox gives up. Jackrabbit finds another pasture. She eats quickly. She listens for more danger.

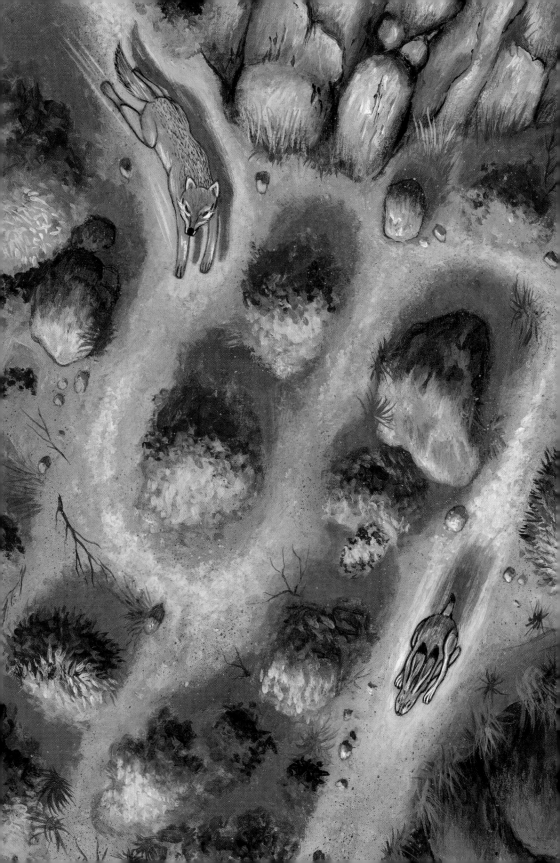

Chapter 3
Time for Sleep

It was a busy night.

Jackrabbit is tired.

She wants to sleep.

She looks for a bush

that will shade her

from the hot sun.

Jackrabbit does not have a burrow. She does not build a nest. Instead, she likes to lie in a low, soft spot. She scratches the ground to make the spot just right. Soon she falls asleep.

Jackrabbit is alert, even when she sleeps. She can always hear sounds of danger. She can hear the sound of a hawk flying. She can hear a coyote walking. If a predator comes too close, she will leave the bush right away.

Chapter 4
Time for Babies

Jackrabbit is now one year old. She has grown quite large. She is about two feet long. She weighs almost eight pounds. She is ready to have babies.

Jackrabbit does not build a nest for the babies she will have. She picks one of her sleeping spots. She places hair in the spot to make it soft.

Early one morning, Jackrabbit has three babies. The babies are born with hair. Their eyes are open. Soon they begin crawling. Jackrabbit nurses her babies.

The babies grow quickly. Jackrabbit continues to nurse them. But she also needs to eat. She cannot stay with her babies while she eats. She must leave them alone.

Before she leaves, Jackrabbit moves each baby to a different spot. She puts one under a bush. She puts one in high grass. She hides one under a fallen tree limb.

When she returns, Jackrabbit calls to her babies. They come to nurse again. In a few weeks, the babies will be on their own. But, for now, they are safe with Jackrabbit.

Glossary

Burrow: a hole or tunnel dug in the ground by an animal.

Pasture: a grassy plot of land used for grazing.

Predator: an animal that hunts other animals.

Wilderness Facts
About the Jackrabbit

Jackrabbits can be found in the southern, western and central United States. They live on prairies, in brush lands and meadows. Many animals and birds hunt jackrabbits. Some of jackrabbits' predators are bobcats, foxes, coyotes, horned owls, badgers, weasels, eagles and snakes.

The jackrabbit is not a rabbit at all. It is a hare. Both rabbits and hares are long-eared mammals, but there are many differences between them. Rabbits are born without hair. Their eyes are closed. Hares are born with hair. Their eyes are open. Rabbits live in burrows. Hares live above ground. A jackrabbit may have four to six litters of babies each year. One female jackrabbit may have eight to twenty-four babies a year.

When running from a predator, jackrabbits flash the white underside of their tails. This may be done to confuse the predator. It might also be a signal of danger to other jackrabbits. A jackrabbit's ears help it adjust to changing temperatures. When hot, it raises its ears to keep cool. When cold, it lays its ears against its body to keep in body heat.

Animals that live near jackrabbits on the prairie include:

Prairie dogs   Swainson's hawks

Roadrunners   Prairie skinks

Hispid pocket mice   Rattlesnakes

Western kingbirds   Coyotes